Tiddlers

Hurry Up!

by Ann Bryant

Illustrated by Terry Pastor

FRANKLIN WATTS
LONDON • SYDNEY

Notes on the series

TIDDLERS are structured to provide support for children who are starting to read on their own. The stories may also be used for sharing with children.

Starting to read alone can be daunting. **TIDDLERS** help by listing the words in the book for a check before reading, and by providing visual support and repeating words and phrases. These books will both develop confidence and encourage reading and rereading for pleasure.

If you are reading this book with a child, here are a few suggestions:

1. Make reading fun! Choose a time to read when you and the child are relaxed and have time to share the story.
2. Talk about the story before you start reading. Look at the cover and the blurb. What might the story be about? Why might the child like it?
3. Look also at the list of words below - can the child tackle most of the words?
4. Encourage the child to retell the story, using the jumbled picture puzzle.
5. Give praise! Remember that small mistakes need not always be corrected.

Here is a list of the words in this story.

Common words:

at	oh	up
no	so	very
off	the	was

Other words:

bus	last	tractor
car	lorry	turned
cross	slow	van
hurry	taxi	

The tractor was very slow.

The car was cross.

The van was cross.

The taxi was
very cross.

So was the lorry.

The bus was very,
very cross.

13

The tractor turned off.

15

At last!

Oh no!

Hurry up, tractor!

Puzzle Time

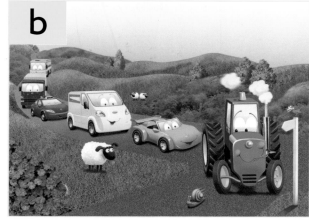

Can you find these pictures in the story?

Which pages are the
pictures from?

Turn over for answers!

Answers

The pictures come from these pages:

a. pages 4 and 5

b. pages 14 and 15

c. pages 8 and 9

d. pages 18 and 19

First published in 2010 by
Franklin Watts
338 Euston Road
London
NW1 3BH

Franklin Watts Australia
Level 17/207 Kent Street
Sydney
NSW 2000

Text © Ann Bryant 2010
Illustration © Terry Pastor 2010

A CIP catalogue record for this book is
available from the British Library.

ISBN 978 0 7496 9389 3 (hbk)
ISBN 978 0 7496 9401 2 (pbk)

Series Editor: Jackie Hamley
Editor: Melanie Palmer
Series Advisor: Catherine Glavina
Series Designer: Peter Scoulding

Printed in China

Franklin Watts is a division of Hachette Children's Books,
an Hachette UK company. www.hachette.co.uk